THE NEW WORLD NEANDERTHALS

They're big...They're brave...They're bold...
THEY'RE BACK!

THE RISE OF THE FORCE

by Gini Graham Scott, Ph.D.

THE NEW WORLD NEANDERTHALS

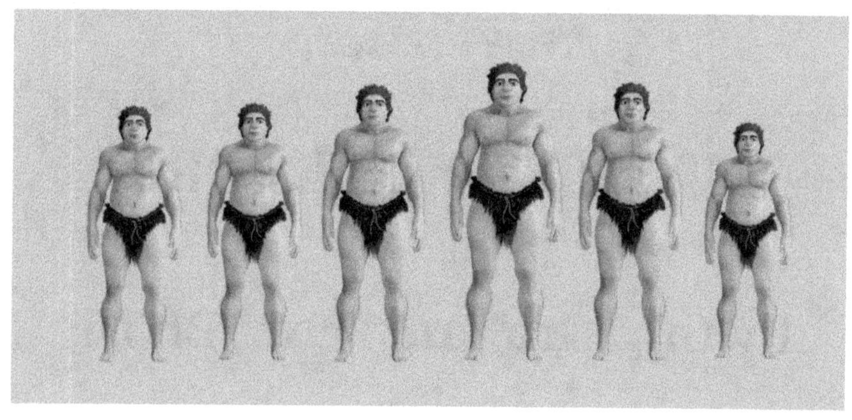

TABLE OF CONTENTS

INTRODUCTION

INTRODUCING THE NEW WORLD NEANDERTHALS

As I started thinking about the Neanderthals, I imagined how the first Neanderthals would return, and I wrote about them in my first book *The Neanderthals Are Back.* This describes how two scientists bring them back through cloning and raise them in a lab with the help of a nursery school teacher. Then, at five or six, they are placed in a group home for kids, later grow up in foster homes, go to school, and as teens and young adults, find jobs doing unskilled work. Along the way, they experience the challenges of everyday life in modern society, though with the added challenge of being Neanderthals.

After writing a series of stories for that book, I wondered what would happen as other groups of scientists bring back more Neanderthals. What would they be like? How could they fit into modern society? And could the qualities that helped them survive for over 100,000 years before becoming extinct help them in modern times? For example, could their strength, aggressiveness, powerful vision, and ability to communicate and coordinate in a hunt turn them into a kind of modern superhero helping the community by using old time skills?

It's those questions that led me to create the New World Neanderthals, who are the central characters in this book.

Who Are the Neanderthals?

The story of the Neanderthals is truly fascinating. There have been hundreds of sites where their bones have been discovered in Europe and Southern and Central South Asia, and these sites contain more than 300 bodies that date back to about 250,000 to 350,000 years ago. The Neanderthals thrived for hundreds of thousands of years, and, for a time, they appear to have lived separately from Homo sapiens until about 100,000 to 30,000 years ago. Sometime during this period, some Neanderthals interbred with humans, so now modern humans have about 2% Neanderthal DNA. Then, suddenly, about 30,000 to 40,000 years ago they went extinct.

But why? The question seems to fascinate scientists who are still debating the reasons, though they commonly express surprise at the Neanderthals' quick extinction. The irony is that the Neanderthals were especially adapted to the cold spell that hit Europe for thousands of years, while modern humans who moved in from Africa and Southern Asia were not. Yet, modern humans thrived, while Neanderthals died off.

Before their disappearance, though, Neanderthals dominated their territory. They were especially strong, fierce hunters, who hunted all types of game, including the mammoth and woolly rhinoceros. They were skilled at hunting in groups and used ambush hunting to trap their prey. They also had a language and the skills to communicate, so they could organize small groups to hunt down game

Mostly they lived in caves in small family groups that combined together into small communities of perhaps 10 to 15 families. They had fire, too. There is evidence that they engaged in cannibalism at times, perhaps after succeeding in a battle with other groups. They appear to have buried their dead in their caves, and even had the beginnings of symbolic thinking and art in the form of handprints in red ochre found in some caves.

Can the Neanderthals Come Back?

Recent developments in extracting DNA from bones using gene editing techniques and cloning show that it really will be possible to bring back Neanderthals. In fact, teams of scientists are working with these technologies to de-extinct once extinct species, such as the Tasmanian tiger, woolly mammoth, and passenger pigeon. As of this writing, they have brought back some animals and are hopeful of bringing back others in the near future.

So far, the research shows it would be possible to create a Neanderthal baby, though scientists have not yet done so.

Taking all of that information together, I imagined that the Neanderthals might have had the brain power of a modern five or six year old. Then, I considered the possibility of bringing the Neanderthals back, which led to *The Neanderthals Are Back* series.

The stories in *The Neanderthals Are Back* show what might happen when Neanderthals grow up in modern society from childhood through young adulthood. Along the way, they go to school, have relationships as teenagers, fall in love with other Neanderthals and sometimes humans, and start working in unskilled jobs. Some even benefit from getting a genius pill which makes them smart for a while. At the same time, like any small distinct population, they face problems of bullying, prejudice, exploitation, and discrimination, though many fight back and some modern humans take up their cause.

Meet the New World Neanderthals

The *New World Neanderthals* continues this story, based on the premise that other scientists in other parts of the country, as well as the world, are bringing back Neanderthals. They might do so for various purposes -- such as to do hard, routine work in factories and fields, as an alternative to bringing in robots. They might do so for entertainment, such as featuring them in boxing and wrestling matches. They might involve them in sports, such as creating a Neanderthal football league.

Then, too, as in these *New World Neanderthal* stories, scientists, community leaders, and government officials might take advantage of the Neanderthals' strength, power, and good vision to use them to aid in police and military activities. In this way, human commanders and coordinators might guide a team of Neanderthals to help with different types of operations where high-tech solutions fail. In fact, they might assist in fighting back against rogue high-tech operations, using their low-tech skills that make them strong and powerful.

These stories are based on the premise that these Neanderthals are first raised in a laboratory setting after they are born where they are taught basic skills, as in *The Neanderthals as Back.* But instead of going to a group home and a regular elementary, middle school, and high school and engaging in low skilled work, they are provided with special training at a young age. Through this training, they are drilled in the basic skills that make the Neanderthals able hunters who can work together as a team to achieve a goal. In Neanderthal times, this goal was a successful hunt. But now, their objective is to assist the police, FBI, or military in some way, where their low-tech skills are needed.

Accordingly, in these stories, the New World Neanderthals are called upon to perform some mission. But can they do it without being exposed, running into danger, or even being killed themselves? Sometimes love appears to provide an antidote to working too hard. Sometimes they face villains, such as corrupt company owners and managers. And sometimes they confront and face off with other Neanderthals who are working for opposing commanders and criminals seeking to score big.

In short, the New World Neanderthal stories are action adventures, as the Neanderthal team members go on different missions and encounter varied challenges. For now, I have written 13 short stories. But I see these tales as the beginning of an expanded series -- as books, as a TV or cable series, or as a film developed from one or more of these stories.

So now, I invite you to meet the New World Neanderthals and experience their stories.

PART I: THE RISE OF THE FORCE

CHAPTER 1: CREATING THE FORCE

When John Montgomery, the head of the AI Research Institute, read about the work of Darryl Jonas with Neanderthals he was intrigued. Jonas had secretly created six Neanderthal kids and raised them in a lab before placing them in a group home, where they lived quietly before the media discovered them.

"How clever," he thought. "Bring the kids back and raise them like ordinary kids in modern society.

He put down the newspaper with the blaring headlines about how one of the kids went exploring only to be hit by a car, after which the cops and then the media arrived.

Montgomery turned to his associate, Dan Hunter, the Research Director.

"Tough luck," he said. "Now the kids will grow up in the spotlight, unless Jonas can figure out some way to keep them away, so the kids can live ordinary lives."

"Yes, so sad," Dan agreed.

"But what if…."

John was thinking now, speculating on what this discovery of Neanderthal kids, created by cloning, could mean for the future of science and technology. He looked out from his window overseeing operations where rows of precision machines turned out an army of robots to work in retail stores and factories. With a flip of a switch or the click of a few buttons on a remote, the robots could file out along the store or factory floor and do any of the simple tasks they had been programmed to do. They could select the correct items from a shelf and put them in a bin to be packaged and shipped to a customer. They could load and unload trucks with supplies or completed projects. They could stand by a conveyer belt and put in selected parts. They could even go out in the fields and plant crops or pull fruit from trees.

He mentally clicked through the many tasks the robots could do. But each simple task required many hours of software development and programming to train the robot to do a particular tasks. Then, if something changed, such as the size of a product going through the conveyor belt or the slope of a field after a heavy rain, the robot had to be programmed again. Yet it was still cheaper than hiring workers at a minimum wage that kept going up and up.

But what if…What if? He imagined there could be dozens of Neanderthals raised and bred to perform such tasks. Then, since Neanderthals were supposed to be strong with relatively low IQs, maybe they would be ideally suited to perform such tasks with no need to pay them.

And what else? What else?

He kept on thinking of the possibilities, as well as the chance to make his own scientific achievement by creating a team of Neanderthal workers.

Just then, Dan Hunter interrupted his thoughts.

"Hey, boss. You've been so quiet and staring into space for a few minutes. What's up?"

John jerked back to the present. He handed the newspaper to Dan and pointed to the headline.

"I was just thinking about how we could do this, too. We could bring in a geneticist or paleontologist to work with us. Then, we could get some Neanderthal DNA and raise some Neanderthal kids ourselves. From an early age, we could start training them, so they could grow up to become workers. And maybe we could put them to work for us."

"What about working for others?" Dan suggested.

"That, too," John said. "You never know what can happen."

And so the seed was planted. John and Dan began exploring the possibility of bringing back their own generation of Neanderthals. They would raise the kids with the help of teachers, sports trainers, and others to be strong and powerful and work together with others as a team. The possibilities seemed endless, as John and Dan thought about all the things they might train their Neanderthals to do.

CHAPTER 2: WORK IT

After 7 years, John thought the Neanderthals might be ready to start working. Alice Miller, who had been teaching them, indicated they could understand basic commands and speak simple sentences. So John called together Dan Hunter and his top managers in the lab into the conference room to explain what they could do.

"Alice is a member of our team of teachers who have been helping the Neanderthals develop basic language and everyday living skills. The teachers are adapting what they teach based on what we know about the behavior and cognitive development of the Neanderthals many thousands of years ago."

"That's right," said Alice. "We know they must have been able to communicate basic information to organize a hunt. And scientists have discovered that they had a hyoid bone, a horseshoe-shaped structure in the throat, like modern humans. So we presume they could speak and had language. The Neanderthals are also believed to be the first cave artists, with some very simple cave art in Cantabria Spain, dating back to about 65,000 years ago, a time before modern humans appeared in Europe around 40,000-45,000 years ago. But it's very simple, only very rough outlines of animals and humans." She projected a slide from her computer on the screen.

“That cave art suggests the Neanderthals had some abilities to think symbolically, but not at the level of modern humans. So that’s how we’ve been teaching the Neanderthal kids -- as if they might have the cognitive abilities of five or six years old.”

“But what if they were taught as if they could learn even more?” Dan asked.

“We don’t know,” John replied. “And we haven’t tried, since we are basically raising the Neanderthals based on their ability to be very strong and aggressive, as well as communicate enough to be on teams. That’s what our investors are interested in -- creating teams of Neanderthals to replace expensive robots powered by artificial intelligence or AI. The robots can become very expensive as the programming becomes more complex. If we can raise the Neanderthals to do this work instead, that’s a big advantage.”

“Understood,” Dan agreed.

“So let Alice continue to explain when we can start having the kids work for us.”

Alice flipped to another slide showing a recreation of a traditional Neanderthal family.

"According to the researchers, it would appear that the children grew up at about the same rate as modern humans, since they had a life span of about 50 years. At about 7 years old, the Neanderthal child might be physically the equivalent to a human child. Yet based on their lack of any written language and their very simple art, we've been estimating that they would have the ability of a five to six year old child."

"But what about their larger brain size," Dan wondered.

"It doesn't matter," said Alice. "It's how the neurons are connected together. Researchers believe the Neanderthals dedicated more of their brains to controlling their bodies, since they were stockier and stronger, and their larger, stronger bodies required more brain control. The Neanderthals also dedicated more of their brain power to vision than modern humans, since the larger eye sockets in their skeletons indicate they had a larger visual cortex than us."

"It's like the circuitry in a computer," Dan commented. "After all, the first computers were very huge, almost the size of a large room. Now the parts are smaller than ever, even microscopic."

"Exactly," said Alice. "That's why we're suggesting that the Neanderthal kids could begin working as young as seven years old. In fact, there are many examples of young kids starting to work and train, such as in family stores and farms, where kids start helping out. Researchers estimate that at seven, the Neanderthals' brain size was about 88% that of an adult compared to the modern human brain size at seven, which is about 95% that of an adult."

"Meaning?" Dan asked.

"Meaning that by seven their brain was pretty much developed, so they could do most of the tasks of an adult, adjusting for their smaller size, of course."

"And that means," John said, "we can easily start putting these kids to work. We can take advantage of their qualities where they are better than humans -- such as their greater strength, aggressiveness, and visual ability. Plus they can work in small groups, and they have some basic communication and language skills, so we can readily teach them what to do. Then, we can use them as best suited to their level of skills and abilities."

And so it was decided. The Neanderthal kids would continue to live in the small group home that was set up for them. It had already been divided into sections corresponding to the work teams of 8 to 12 Neanderthals.

John thought these arrangements ideal, because in the past few years, the Neanderthals had spent several hours a day with Alice, learning some basic words and sentences, so they could understand simple instructions and talk to each other. Occasionally, she had invited them to experiment with using brushes and paints to draw simple outlines and shapes, such as appeared in the early cave art by Neanderthals or early humans.

Then, too, they had had a chance to play in the grassy backyard behind the lab, which had high walls so no one driving by could see them. Mostly their play consisted of running around, playing tag and hide and seek, throwing balls, and jumping up and down, much like dogs and cats might play with each other. They had sometimes used plastic or foam spears and hammers as if they were back in the woods hunting down bears and mammoths. And sometimes John had let in some chickens or wild game for them to chase, after which the Neanderthals and staff members had enjoyed cooking the meat for dinner over a campfire.

As John explained when the experiment started: "I want to recreate Neanderthal times as much as possible while the kids are growing up."

But now it was time to continue the experiment and put the kids to work. John had high hopes of the possibility.

As he and Dan led Alice out of the conference room, he commented: "I think we're really onto something here. It'll be a real breakthrough. Just think. If we can show that the Neanderthal kids make great workers, we can raise more and more kids and have Neanderthal teams working everywhere. It'll be a whole new workforce for the 21st century -- and we were the first to come up with the idea."

CHAPTER 3: THE BIG PAYOFF

Ten years later, John Montgomery stood with Dan Hunter in their shipping department watching the Neanderthals work. At one time, the company had nearly a hundred robots scurrying from shelf to shelf picking up packages. As needed, their team of AI specialists repeatedly changed the programming, so the robots would go to different shelves or pick up more than one package for multiple orders. At times, the specialists fixed the circuitry when robots somehow collided with each other.

As John commented to Dan as they watched: "Just think how much we are saving now. The transition really works. Before we not only had the cost of creating the robots, but then we had the cost of the programmers programming them. And if things went wrong, the AI guys had to program the robots again."

"That's right," Dan agreed. "And don't forget the replacement costs when robots crashed into each other and couldn't be fixed. Or the costs of replacing merchandise, when the programming went haywire and the robots knocked over some shelves."

"I know. But the Neanderthals are so much more careful. And they know to pick up things and put them back."

"They don't crash into each other either."

"No they don't. They're definitely more cost effective. And I like their strength. You don't have to worry about them breaking under too much weight, since they bring in another Neanderthal or two to help them lift or move things. Like a real team."

"You can't program the robots to do that."

"No," said John, his cheek swelling with pride. "The Neanderthals are a great team. And they're our team."

John and Dan fell silent as they continued watching the Neanderthal team in action.

A few minutes later, the 5 p.m. whistle blew and the Neanderthals working on the floor stopped and filed out, while another Neanderthal team filed in. Soon they had scattered around the warehouse and began working. John turned proudly back to Dan.

"Sure, we need two or three teams for shifts, so the Neanderthals can get some sleep and have some time off to be with their friends, like they're a family. So they need some break times, while the robots can work continuously for days or weeks until their circuitry gets too hot and they have to cool down."

"Or they crash and break down," Dan added.

"Yes, that, too," said John. "But even with all the food and meal breaks, the Neanderthals still are more cost effective, since we don't have to pay them. Just keep them fit and healthy, so they can stay well and strong."

John beamed as he looked down on the shipping floor.

"They've been doing a great job in our factory, too."

As John talked, another team of Neanderthals were working in the factory, where they pulled parts off an assembly line and put them together to create a mechanical toy.

"So you might say they're the perfect work force. They take direction well and seem to learn quickly. Then, they do whatever we ask them to do."

"Or what others ask of them."

"Of course. We just have to introduce them to their new leader and train them to do what he or she wants. So now, if we can just keep our work with them secret for a little longer, we can continue to get new accounts without any competition. Let's let everyone think we are just creating robots for them, and we should do fine."

Just then John's secretary called on his mobile phone. "The company interested in your robots is here," she said.

"Good. Dan and I will be right down," John said.

He clicked the phone off and turned to Dan.

"Our meeting. Is all the paperwork in order?"

Dan nodded and they went down the corridor to the main building.

The client, Stan Bigelow, and two associates, Frank and Rick, were already seated in the conference room. Dan pulled out three agreement forms and handed them to Stan and his associates.

"What's this?" Stan asked.

"An NDA," John said. "You need to sign it before we discuss anything."

"But why? We're just here to get some robots for our factory. Nothing secret about that. You advertise them everywhere, promote them at trade shows."

"Yes, but you wanted to know how you can save money with our newer robot program. And we have something top secret to show you."

Stan glared down at the contract, jumped up, and glared at John angrily.

"But it says we could be liable for millions of dollars if we share what you tell us. That's highway robbery."

"Not if you don't say anything," said John. "We just want to make sure our project stays secret until we are ready to announce this to the world. So we only show it selectively to certain handpicked clients or referrals."

Stan relaxed and sat back down. He looked at the agreement again.

"But you haven't shown me anything yet. Am I obligated to get it if I don't like it."

"No, not at all. Just be quiet about anything we show you. Don't tell anyone. Not even your wife or kids. This secret has to remain confidential, so it's only known to those invited into this room for our special presentation and to everyone working on this project"

"That's right," said Dan firmly. "This has been our company's trade secret for 10 years, and we intend to keep it that way."

"Okay, okay," said Stan, signing reluctantly.

He passed the agreement to his two associates who signed, too. Then, he passed their signed agreement to John.

"All right," said John scooping up the agreements. "Let's begin, and I'll show you what our big secret program is all about."

A few minutes later, John, Dan, Stan and his associates were in the small control center overlooking the warehouse.

"This is it," said John, pointing to the warehouse floor, where a few dozen Neanderthals were rushing back and forth picking up boxes from the shelves and filling them up with different items for shipment."

"But those aren't robots," Stan exclaimed. "You have people working on the shelves."

"No. Not ordinary people," John replied. "They're Neanderthals. And it turns out they're cheaper and more efficient than humans or robots. Now you can have them working for you, too, as long as you see the value and keep who you hire secret."

"Or lose millions if you sue us," said Stan grimly.

"No. Make millions if you work with us," John countered. "So are you in? Do you want a team of Neanderthals working with you in your factory? We'll provide the training and instructions for dealing with the Neanderthals. We'll tell you everything you need to be successful, and within a few weeks you'll see how your costs go down and your profits go up."

"It's a win-win solution for you," said Dan.

"You just have to keep it secret," said John.

Stan reached out his hand.

"Okay. A deal. I'll pay you for each Neanderthal worker, take care of them, and put them to work like you say. And like you say, I'll keep the project secret."

John extended his hand and shook hands with Stan.

"Very good. We have a deal."

Then, John, Dan, Stan, and his associates looked down at the shipping warehouse, as the Neanderthal workers continued to walk or run around quickly to find the right items, fill up packages, and put them on the conveyer belt.

"And look over there. As you can see for yourself," said John, "they continue to work so quickly and do their tasks with a kind of military precision. Now, you'll have them doing that for you, too."

"Yeah, that's what I like about this," Stan commented. "Having a great team to work for us. Thanks for letting us in on your secret operation. And if this works well, we'll want to order many more. Yes, many, many more."

CHAPTER 4: CREATING EVEN MORE NEANDERTHALS

After Stan and his associates left, John smiled broadly at Dan, who was sitting nearby.

"Well, we did it," John exclaimed. "Our biggest contract yet. One million. And we can expand even more if we can clone and breed our Neanderthal workers quickly enough."

"I'll check into it," said Dan, "and I'll look for a few more barracks or warehouses we can set up with beds. I have a few scientists in Germany, France, and Spain working on getting the DNA for us from different burial sites. And they're willing to give up some DNA for research purposes."

"Wonderful. It's a good thing we set up that non-profit foundation for DNA research."

"Yes," said Dan. "For medical and health improvements."

"Exactly. And that's true. Nobody needs to know how we're using the discoveries to create a Neanderthal workforce."

"And they won't," said Dan. "Not even our security guards, administrators, or medical staff know what this is all about."

"Good. We've been able to do this for ten years, so now we just need to keep doing what we've been doing. Then, everything should work out fine."

John pulled out a bottle of wine from a cabinet on the wall.

"So let's celebrate," he said, popping the cork.

He poured two glasses of wine and gave one to Dan.

"To continued success in spreading the Neanderthal work teams everywhere."

Dan laughed. "Yeah. To success. It'll be like the way they spread around Europe and Asia thousands of years ago."

"Right," said John holding his glass up high. "But now they aren't just spreading as they follow and hunt their game. Instead, it's a whole new game, and we're in charge and winning the game."

John and Dan clicked their glasses together and laughed as they raised them to their lips and savored the wine.

After that, Dan went downstairs to check over operations. Everything seemed to be running so smoothly. The conveyor belts were running by quickly with packages. The Neanderthals were going around as they had been instructed to find packages with colored dots that represented numbers for different items. He was pleased they had even learned to identify a series of 8 to 12 numbers, so they could distinguish different items and place the correct ones in a large package for shipping.

He also noticed their agility in climbing ladders to reach items on the higher shelves, while the robots had difficulty getting objects from them, since most couldn't see that high and reach with their arms at the same time. He was impressed, too, by their strength, since they could carry more items and much larger, heavier items than humans could.

Then, it was time for the Neanderthals' meal break. One of the floor supervisors rang the bell to let them know it was time to get their bowls of meat and bread from the mechanical cart that rolled up and down the aisle. It stopped when one or more Neanderthals came close to it to get their lunch or dinner.

Dan watched them eat standing in small groups, and when another bell rang after 15 minutes, they dutifully returned to finding packages and putting them on the conveyor belt.

"Good," he thought to himself, "everything's running so perfectly.

Then, for a moment, Dan worried: "What could possibly go wrong?" But he quickly brushed the thought away, as he turned the operations over to Jack Burns, the night shift manager, and stopped by John's office behind the shipping facility.

"I'm off now. Everything's fine, so don't work too hard," Dan said.

John looked up from the budget and cash projections he was reviewing.

"Oh, don't worry about that," he called back playfully. "I never do."

Then, as he looked at the projections, he imagined teams of Neanderthals replicating themselves as they got hired doing all kinds of tasks he imagined they could do. He could picture them working on farms instead of humans and mechanical pickers. They could work on road construction crews all over the U.S. and in Alaska and Canada, and better withstand the cold than humans. They might work with loggers clearing the forests in designated areas to reduce fire danger and provide more land for farming and mining. Maybe they could even join teams of wrestlers and boxers to add a new dimension to the sport.

Yes, there were so many things that he imagined the Neanderthals could do if there were enough of them. "But give it time," he thought. "Just give us some more time, and our company can produce more and more Neanderthals."

He imagined the company just needed seven years for each new generation, and so far his company was the only one producing Neanderthal workers. "If only we can keep it that way," he thought, as he looked at more budget projections, and saw the millions upon millions of dollars adding up.

CHAPTER 5: RECRUITING THE FORCE

A few days later, when the shipping operations were humming along as usual, John was going over records in his office when Jane Winston, the receptionist at the front desk, called him on the intercom.

"There are some men here who want to speak to you."

John glanced at his calendar.

"I wasn't expecting anyone."

"They said it's important."

John frowned, annoyed.

"Well, tell them they have to set up an appointment. Everyone thinks whatever they want to discuss is important. I need to know what they want to talk about so I can prepare."

Jane got ready to shoo the men away and began telling them: "The CEO is busy now. But he'd like me to find out more about what you want so I can set up a meeting."

"Make it now," one of the men said, and he flashed a badge.

Jane called John back.

"They're from the local police force. They're detectives," she said.

John held the intercom silently for a few moments, stunned and suddenly scared.

"Did they say why they're here?" he said.

"No. Just that they want to talk to you now."

John glanced nervously at the photo of the Neanderthals working in the warehouse.

"God, what do they want?" he worried, as he imagined the worst. Maybe the detectives had somehow heard about the Neanderthal workers and now had all kinds of charges in mind -- hiring undocumented workers, having them work in unsafe conditions, or not paying wages, so maybe this could be considered human slavery. But then he could explain how he had treated them very well and humanely by providing meal breaks, education, and plenty of time between shifts for relaxation and recreation. So what could the problem be?

Then, he heard Jane's voice again saying "Sir?" and he jerked out of his reverie.

"Okay. Go ahead. Send them up," he said.

He adjusted his tie and sat up straight to look as professional and businesslike as possible.

Then, a knock on the door.

"Come in," he said.

Three men in matching blue suit jackets and ties strode in.

"I'm Lieutenant Jack Davis with the investigative detective unit of the Franklin P.D.," he said. "And this is Sergeant Don Burrows and Sergeant Will Garrett."

The detectives sat down in three chairs across from John.

"We heard about your Neanderthals," Lt. Davis said, "and we wanted to talk to you about that."

John felt beads of sweat form on his forehead, and he hoped the detectives didn't notice how scared he was.

"Uhhh, how did you hear about them?" John asked.

"We can't tell you," Lt. Davis said. "We just learned they were working for you in your shipping department."

John nodded. "Yes, that's true."

He flashed back to his meeting a few days before with Stan and his associates signing a million dollar contract. Was that how the detectives knew? Was Stan a spy for them? If so, was the million dollar contract just a ploy to get information and get him convicted of some crime? Then, how did Stan find out about the Neanderthals, since he was so careful to work on referrals only. Who else might have shared this information?

"If you can tell us more about what they are doing for you, that would be helpful," Lt. Davis said.

At once, John snapped back to their conversation.

"What do you want to know? What's wrong? Maybe I should bring in my lawyer before I talk to you? Am I…under arrest?"

Lt. Davis and his two associates laughed.

"Oh, no," Lt. Davis said. "We're not here to charge you with anything. We thought maybe you could help us, and maybe we could hire some Neanderthals, too."

"What?"

John sat back stunned, not sure what to say.

"That's right. We're working undercover on some cases, where we could use some help. So, of course, any work they do for us will be confidential. No one else will know. Not even the officers in other departments or the higher ups in the police force. We'll just call them confidential informants, if that's okay with you?"

"Okay with me? With me?" John thought. He could hardly believe what the officers were saying. He wasn't in trouble, and they were offering him a deal. He could barely think of what to say or do, so he just sat silently, thinking about how to respond.

"And we'll pay them, of course," Lt. Davis said. "Or pay you, and you can take care of their compensation."

"Yes, that'll be fine," John managed.

"Okay, then, we agree," Lt. Davis said. "We'll work out the details and send you a contract. We'd like to start with six Neanderthals. We thought they might make a good squad."

"Of course," John agreed.

"And please, pick out your best men for the job. What we need are guys that are strong, aggressive, have really good vision, and can work well together as a group, like Neanderthals do when out on a hunt. At least that's what we read about them."

John nodded, amazed as he listened.

"Because that's what we want them for. We're on a hunt for one really bad criminal who escaped from prison, and we've got him located in the desert near some mountains and caves. But our guys don't have the skills or smarts to go there. So when we heard about the Neanderthals, we thought that's it. A perfect fit. They can go there to find him, and it's something we can't do."

Lt. Davis laughed. "And of course we can't send in any robots to do this. We need some actual humans to go there, or more precisely some humans with the kinds of qualities the Neanderthals are known for. So what do you say? Can we do this together?"

"Yes, yes," said John, trying to contain his mounting excitement so he wouldn't seem too eager, as he negotiated the terms of the deal. "I'd like to do that, and I think we can all make a good team."

"Very good," said Lt. Davis. "And remember, this assignment has to be hush hush. No one can know. At least for now, while the Neanderthals do their first assignment. Otherwise, the top brass and others in the department could think we're crazy and out of line. But the guys in our undercover unit talked about it, and we feel sure it'll work."

Lt. Davis and his associates got up. He reached across the table and shook hands with John.

"Okay, then. We'll talk more in the next few days and I'll bring over the contract. We'll have lots to discuss about our plans for this first operation."

He paused at the door.

"Oh, and lets call this Neanderthal team something. How about the New Force? It is new, though a little ironic isn't it, since these guys go back many thousands of years.

He chuckled as he and his associates walked through the door and John watched them go.

The New Force, he thought to himself. The New Force. Nice, straightforward, and simple. He thought the Neanderthal team he selected would like it, too.

PART II: THE NEW FORCE IN ACTION

CHAPTER 6: FINDING THE FIRST SIX

A few days after signing the contract, Lt. Davis and Sergeants Burrows and Garrett met with John and Dan to tour the shipping facility, so they could select the six Neanderthals for the force. As they walked around, the Neanderthal workers rushed around as usual selecting items, putting them in packages and on the conveyer belt.

"We want the best individuals from your facility for this assignment," Lt. Davis explained. "You know, the best of your best."

"Understood," John said.

He pointed out different Neanderthals as they walked around, referring to them by the numbers on the back of their loose fitting shirts.

"That's how we keep track of them," Dan said. "That way we can know who's where and what they are doing."

"The numbers are fine," Lt. Davis replied. "But once we select them, we'll give them names. We want them to feel a special pride at being chosen for this elite unit."

"And that'll breed loyalty, too," Sgt. Burrows added. "To each other and the whole unit."

"Well, we used numbers because there are so many of them," John replied a little defensively. "But we treat them really well. With plenty of good food, and time for breaks, sleep, and recreation."

"Of course," Lt. Davis said, reassuringly. "We'll be using them for special assignments. So we want to do that little bit extra, so they'll be good loyal soldiers. We want to build esprit de corps."

They continued walking, and from time to time, John pointed out one of the stand-out Neanderthals.

"That's 2604," he said, as they stopped by a Neanderthal putting large TVs in boxes. "He's really strong. So we use him for especially big packages."

"Good," said Lt. Davis. "We'll add him to the group. And we'll give him a name. What about Adam, since he's the first?"

"Then, Adam it is," said John, making a note that 2604 would now be called Adam.

John motioned for Adam to finish packing up a TV and come with them.

"You'll be joining Lt. Davis for a special job," John said.

"Okay, yes, sir," Adam said, stepping behind Lt. Davis.

The group walked on past a few rows of shelves to the conveyer belt. They stopped behind a Neanderthal with the number 3048 on his shirt.

"This is 3048," John said. "He's been especially alert when there have been problems with the conveyers slowing down or packages bunching up. Then, he signals the human supervisor to speed up the belt or stop it."

"Sounds like just what we need," said Lt. Davis. "Invite him to join the group. And let's call him Brad, since he's the second to join us. If we use the ABCs, it'll be easier to remember everyone's name."

"So noted," said John, making the notation on his list of Neanderthal numbers and corresponding names.

Brad left his station by the conveyer belt and stepped into the group beside Adam.

Then, John continued leading the group around the shipping facility, pointing out different Neanderthals he thought did an especially good job at something.

At the end of the tour, six Neanderthals were lined up in two rows behind Lt. Davis and Sergeants Burrows and Garrett -- Adam, Brad, Charlie, Derrick, Eddy, and Fred.

John led everyone into his office behind the shipping facility.

"Have a seat everyone," he said.

He motioned for everyone to sit down around the conference table.

The Neanderthals looked around, gazing at the walls, tables, and everyone at the table with amazement, since they had never seen such a room before.

John smiled broadly at each of the Neanderthals to show they were welcome and this was a supportive, friendly meeting. He spoke slowly, with the simple words the Neanderthals had learned in their training when they were growing up and when they began working in the facility.

"You'll be joining a new special group. You'll go with Lt. Davis. He'll take care of you and train you for your new job."

He paused, to check that the Neanderthals were following his explanation, then continued.

"You will have new names, too. They will be names like humans have. No more numbers."

The Neanderthals grinned as he spoke.

"Good, they seem to see this is an honor," John thought.

He pointed to each Neanderthal in turn.

"You're Adam…You're Brad…You're Charlie…You're Derrick…You're Eddy…You're Fred."

The Neanderthals nodded as John named them, and then he continued.

"Now you'll be going with Lt. Davis. He will have special work for you. You'll like it. You will learn new skills. You will work together as a group. You will live in a new place just for you. And it will be fun."

Again, John paused, making sure the Neanderthals understood and would go along with whatever Lt. Davis planned for them.

For a few moments, the Neanderthals signaled to each other with hand signs and smiles.

Then, Adam, spoke. "Yes. We know. It'll be good. We like to learn."

John, Dan, Lt. Davis and the sergeants leaned back, relieved that the changeover seemed to go smoothly, much better than they had thought. They were pleased that the Neanderthals understood, liked what they were doing, and could even speak.

"Very good," said John. "Now follow Lt. Davis and he'll take you to your new home and job."

Lt. Davis and the sergeants stood up, and Lt. Davis motioned for the Neanderthals to follow him. Pushing their chairs behind them, the Neanderthals formed a line as they followed Lt. Davis and the sergeants out the door. Adam walked in front, followed by Brad, then Charlie, and lastly by Derrick, Eddy, and Fred.

John marveled at how they followed the detectives out in a line. It was as if each Neanderthal knew his place and was ready to follow the leader, based on the order in which they had been chosen.

"I'll keep you posted on how everything is going," Lt. Davis called back.

"Thanks," John said and watched a little wistfully as the group left. He had grown fond of the Neanderthals and would miss the ones he sent away.

But then he looked down at the signed contract on the table with the first $10,000 payment for the six workers, and he felt better already.

"It'll be fine," he thought to himself. "It's gonna be fine."

CHAPTER 7: TRAINING DAYS

Once in front of the shipping facility, the Neanderthals got into the cars with the detectives, two in each of their cars. Lt. Davis led the convoy to the small house in the country, where they would live and train over the next few weeks. Once they were ready, they would get their first assignment.

The house was located in a clearing in the woods at the end of a windy narrow road that snaked off from the main highway. Lt Davis thought the location ideal, because he wanted someplace very private, so he could keep the program secret from the top brass and others in the department. And he certainly didn't want the media to know, since the Neanderthal project was a pilot program. He wanted to be sure it would work, before unveiling it to higher ups or the world.

As Lt. Davis drove, he shifted his glance back and forth from the road to watching Adam and Brad in the back seat. They looked around eagerly, fascinated by all the cars around them as they sped along the freeway. When Lt. Davis turned onto the side road, they became even more excited as they saw the trees hugging the side of the road.

Excitedly, they spun around, looking at the side windows and then out back, pointing their fingers and speaking quickly to each other in short phrases.

"Look, trees."

"Green plants."

"Red flowers."

"And see the big rocks."

"So many trees."

Lt. Davis was glad to hear them talking. That would make teaching them even easier if they already understood basic words and short sentence. Then, he could teach them more.

Finally, the house with dark brown wooden planks appeared in the distance.

"We're almost there," he told Adam and Brad.

Once they arrived, the other two cars with the other four Neanderthals pulled in behind them. Lt. Davis waved for the others to follow him to the house.

Inside, he led the Neanderthals to their three bedrooms, each about 12x15 feet with two bunk beds, The Neanderthals quickly divided up, two to a room, as if they already knew the drill. Adam and Brad took the first bedroom, Charlie and Derrick took the second, Eddy and Fred took the third, and the first man in each group took the bottom bunk.

"Amazing," said Lt. Davis to Sergeants Burrows and Garrett, as the Neanderthals settled in. "They're already so disciplined, like a military unit. Just think if we took six random guys off a factory floor and brought them here. It would be chaos as they fought each other for the best room and lower bunk."

"Yeah, I noticed that," said Sgt. Burrows. "Having this military spirit will certainly help when we train them."

"And when we assign them to help with an investigation, such as finding and catching a criminal," Sgt. Garrett added.

"Exactly," said Lt. Davis. "Maybe they can help us with the things we can't do ourselves."

"Let's hope so," Sgt. Burrows agreed. "Otherwise..."

Lt. Davis interrupted him. "Don't worry. Whatever the outcome, we'll find a way to bury whatever we spend in the budget. It'll be our secret for now. Then if the training works out, we'll introduce them to the rest of the detective squad."

* * * * * *

The following day, the training began, led by Lt. Davis and the two sergeants. The plan was to teach the Neanderthals basic outdoor and indoor skills for following suspects, discovering where they were hiding, flushing them out, and ultimately trapping them. Then, the cops could arrest them and bring them in.

As the Neanderthals gathered in the living room, as a fire burned in the fireplace, Lt. Davis explained the basics.

"We'll be teaching you some new skills. We'll start with what you already know how to do. We'll learn what you are good at. Then, we'll help you get even better. That way you can help us. Sound good?"

The Neanderthals nodded. "Yes, sir," they said, almost in unison.

"Then let us begin."

Soon after that, Lt. Davis and the sergeants began training them. They divided the Neanderthals into two groups and showed them how to run around the woods and find where members of the other group were hiding. They demonstrated how to sneak up on others, tag them, and tie ropes around them to capture them, much like they might sneak up on a deer or panther in the wild. The detectives also gave them spears modeled after the spears Neanderthals once used and invited them to throw them at targets. They showed them new ways to communicate with each other by using whistles that sounded like bird calls.

They then asked the Neanderthals what they might do if they were chasing someone who didn't want to be caught.

"We can trap him," said Adam.

He and Brad then demonstrated how Adam might come from one direction, Brad from another. If they needed more help, Charlie and Derrick might appear from still another direction, while Eddy and Fred might wait in hiding. This way, as a team, they could capture the person when he tried to run away.

Day after day, the Neanderthals kept practicing different moves, and Lt. Davis noticed how the Neanderthals ran faster and faster and grew stronger and stronger as they worked out. They especially liked to charge their opponent with simple natural weapons, such as sticks, rocks, and even dirt which they could pick up and throw. But they could use modern weapons, too, such as when Lt. Davis handed them a baton, throwing stick, boomerang, or stick with a ball and chain, and they charged with it or threw it. The more they practiced, the better they became at hitting their targets or capturing the straw dummies that Lt. Davis and the sergeants used to simulate the criminals they hunted.

Finally, after several weeks of practicing different techniques, Lt. Davis decided they were ready.

"Now let's see if they can help us for real," he told Sergeants Burrows and Garrett.

"What do you mean?" Sgt. Burrows asked.

"Well, I was thinking about a prison escapee who is still hiding out in the dessert or the mountains. The police have given up on him. But maybe the Neanderthals can track him down and capture him. We sure haven't able to do that ourselves. We can't even find him."

So that's how it started -- putting the Neanderthals to work on an actual case.

When Lt. Davis told the Neanderthals their plans, they were excited.

"Sounds very good," said Adam.

"I like it," said Brad.

"And it'll be very cool, as you say," said Charlie.

Lt. Davis thought the Neanderthals were more than ready. They had even been picking up on their own speech patterns. Now what could they do in the field? Lt. Davis and Sergeants Burrows and Garrett were eager to find out.

CHAPTER 8: THE FIRST MISSION

Early the next morning, Lt. Davis, flanked by Sgt. Burrows and Sgt. Garrett, met in the Neanderthals' cabin. The Neanderthals, wearing light blue shirts and jeans, stood in the living room in a semi-circle in front of him, like a military unit awaiting their orders.

"Okay. We have a project for you," Lt. Davis said. 'It will show what you can do. It's for real this time."

The Neanderthals listened quietly, like soldiers awaiting more details.

"Do you understand?"

The Neanderthals nodded in unison.

Lt. Davis continued. "Okay. We have to find this guy. He killed people and escaped from prison."

Lt. Davis held up a picture of the prisoner and passed it to Adam, who looked at it, passed it to Brad, who similarly looked at it and passed it on. After Fred, the last in line, looked at it, he brought it back to Lt. Davis.

"Okay. That's who you will look for," Lt. Davis said. "You'll have these weapons if you need them. And some water, too."

Sgt. Burrows and Sgt. Garrett stepped forward with six backpacks. Sgt. Burrows opened one of them and placed the contents on the floor beside it -- a baton, a throwing stick, a hunting boomerang, a stick with a ball and chain, and some rocks -- the same weapons they had been practicing with. Then, Sgt. Garrett stepped forward with six spears and gave one to each Neanderthal.

"In case you want to use this," Lt. Davis said. "Just think of this search like hunting for game."

The Neanderthals smiled happily as Lt. Davis continued. "You just have to find him for us. Then, you have to surround him. You want to keep him where he is."

"That's so he can't get away," Sgt. Burrows added.

"Trap him?" Adam asked.

"That's right," Lt. Davis said. "Trap him and hold him there."

"Then, we'll come and get him," Sgt. Garrett added.

"Yes, do that," said Lt. Davis. "Or maybe bring him to us. Either way, we'll take it from there."

Adam glanced around at the other Neanderthals, who each nodded in turn.

"Okay. We do it. We help you. We want to help," Adam said.

With that, the meeting was over.

Lt. Davis and Sergeants Burrows and Garrett led the Neanderthals to their cars parked on the road to the cabin. The Neanderthals, carrying their spears and backpacks, got in, just as they had before -- Adam and Brad in the first car with Lt. Davis, Charlie and Derrick in the next car with Sgt. Burrows, and finally Eddy and Fred in the last car with Sgt. Garrett.

Then, the cars sped off, heading toward the road through the desert where the prison escapee was last seen.

* * * * * *

A few hours later, the cars were driving on a narrow dirt road that ran alongside a wide expanse of desert. In the distance, the spikes of rocky hills and mountains shot up, looking like a barren moonscape. An old Ford pickup truck was parked in the dirt by the roadside, and a few footsteps led away from it in the mud. A few feet out, the sands of the desert covered up any prints.

Lt. Davis stopped behind the truck and got out of his car, followed by the sergeants and Neanderthals. As the Neanderthals assembled in a row in front of him, Sgt. Burrows and Sgt. Garrett joined him, one standing on either side.

"This is where we need you to find the prisoner," he said to the Neanderthals.

He turned to Sgt. Burrows and Sgt. Garrett and pointed to the truck. "This is where the prisoner abandoned his stolen truck, since he ran out of gas. So he's probably somewhere out there, since no one picked him up. About a week ago, the department got a call about this abandoned stolen truck."

Lt. Davis turned back to the Neanderthals. He pointed to the tracks in the mud leading to the desert.

"He's out there somewhere. His tracks end here."

The Neanderthals gathered around him to look at the tracks.

"So you go out there," Lt. Davis continued. "See if you can find him."

"We try," Adam said.

Lt. Davis reached in his pocket and pulled out a cell phone. He reached out to hand it to Adam, telling him.

"You can reach us on this phone. Call us if you need help. Or call if you find him. I'll show you how it works."

But Adam pushed his hand away.

"No. We do it our way. We find him. We capture him for you."

Lt. Davis pulled back his hand with the phone.

"Okay. Do it your way. And come back if you don't find him, too."

Adam glanced around, as the other Neanderthals nodded their agreement.

"Okay. We will," Adam said.

"And good luck to all of you," Lt. Davis said.

As the Neanderthals set off, Lt. Davis the sergeants waved, and the Neanderthals waved back.

As he watched them walk away on the steaming hot sands, Lt. Davis worried. What if they got lost and didn't come back? What if they found the criminal and he shot one or more of them dead? What if they succumbed to the desert heat? What if?

He turned to Sgt. Burrows and Sgt. Garrett.

"I was just thinking whether we should be doing this? After all, these guys will be exposed in the desert to all the elements. And Adam wouldn't even take my cell phone in case they need any help."

"Look, don't worry. These guys are pretty strong and resourceful," Sgt. Burrows said.

"And at least this project is still secret. So no one else but us knows about it, if things go south," said Sgt. Garrett.

"That's what worries me, too," Lt. Davis said. "No one else knows about this. So we can't call on anyone in the department for help. And the prison has already given up on finding their escaped prisoner in the desert. It's too expensive to search, and if he doesn't turn up anywhere else, they think he's dead."

"So we just have to wait," said Sgt. Burrows.

"Yeah, we just wait," Lt. Davis agreed.

CHAPTER 9: KEEP ON TRACKING

Adam and the other Neanderthals waved back as they walked away. Then, they looked around at the sands that stretched out like a bumpy carpet and at the rock strewn hills and mountains in the distance. A few lumpy white clouds fluttered by in the light blue sky.

Suddenly, it felt very freeing to be outside that musty cabin or in the woods that surrounded the cabin like a wall of trees. It had felt freeing to run around in the woods playing hide and seek and "I found you" games. But the time outside soon ended, and they were back in the cabin that felt like a prison with its small rooms and stacked up bunk beds.

Now here they were ready to do what they loved doing best -- go hunting for something, anything. And if they could help their masters, Lt. Davis and the two sergeants, that was even better.

"Look!" Adam called out and pointed to the spot where the track seemed to end where the mud turned to sand.

The other Neanderthals gathered around him to look closely at the disappearing footprints.

"We have to find where they go," Adam said. "Man out there somewhere."

Adam pointed to the wide expense of desert and rocks.

"So we look hard. We find."

Adam took a stick from his backpack. He pushed some of the sand away from where the footprints disappeared.

"See. Some footprints still there. We can follow."

Adam moved more sand aside, as the other Neanderthals followed behind him. With the sand removed, Adam saw the faint imprint of a trail the detectives hadn't seen.

The footprints went on for about a mile, a continuing trail left under the sand. Then, it stopped.

Adam and the other Neanderthals looked around. What happened? They looked around, and the sand sparkled in the sun like a large lake surrounded by rocky mountains on one side and a few trees by the road on the other.

"Let's rest and think what could happen," Adam said.

The others sat down around him. They dug into their backpacks, drank from their canteens, and ate some of the nuts and berries Lt. Davis and the sergeants had packed for them.

"Maybe wind. Maybe rain," Adam said finally. "So maybe we have to look further."

The other Neanderthals agreed, and soon they pushed the sand aside in ever widening circles. Meanwhile, the hot desert sun bore down on them. They found collapsible straw hats in their backpacks and put them on, though they still sweated in the fierce desert heat.

Finally, Brad pushed aside some sand and noticed some tracks.

"We found them!" he cried out, and everyone gathered around the soft heel impressions in the ground.

"Good, we dig through the sand here," Adam said.

So they continued pushing the sand aside in their new location. On and on they dug through the sand until the tracks led to the rocks and craggy hills surrounding the desert.

"We're here. He's somewhere here," Adam announced. "No more footprints in the rocks. But we still find him."

Three of the Neanderthals started to move ahead towards the rocks.

"No, wait!" Adam called out. "We must go slowly. We must plan. We have to see him first before he sees us."

So the Neanderthals gathered in a circle by the entrance to the rocks and hills, as the late afternoon sun sank lower in the sky and the shadows deepened. They welcomed the growing coolness and coming darkness.

"This will help us," Adam told everyone. "We just have to wait a little longer. We see if he's somewhere. Then, we find him, bring him in."

Meanwhile, Lt. Davis and the sergeants waited nervously by the truck, wondering what was happening.

"We'll be on assignment a little bit longer," Lt. Davis called in to headquarters. But he didn't tell the officer who answered what the assignment was.

CHAPTER 10: UNDER THE COVER OF DARKNESS

As the darkness settled in, Adam urged everyone to wait a little longer.

"We wait now till best," he said. "And we stay quiet. No one must hear us."

So they all sat quietly, resting on their haunches or sitting on the desert floor.

Soon the moon rose slowly in the eastern sky. It was only a three quarter moon, not as bright as a full moon, but its light cast an eerie glow across the rocks. Though Lt. Davis had put flashlights in their packs, the Neanderthals didn't want to use them, not wanting to show anyone where they were. Instead, they could travel silently in the faint light of the moon.

When the moon was about halfway up in the sky, Adam signaled to the others.

"Okay. Everyone ready. We can go."

"But how find him?" Brad asked.

"We just look, watch. Look for animals moving. Maybe they call out to others. Maybe birds circle if he's hurt, bleeding. So we move slowly. Watch."

Waving for the others to follow, Adam moved through the first circle of rocks on the ground towards the rocky hills and outcroppings.

Then he stopped, and so did the others. Now they listened and looked for any signs of where the prisoner might be hiding, if he was still in the rocky hills somewhere.

Suddenly, a fox appeared, its eyes glistening yellow in the moonlight. It stared at the Neanderthals, and they stared back. Unnerved, the fox loped away.

Then came a coyote and wolf. They each stopped about 25 feet away behind a wall of boulders and bushes, watching the Neanderthals with fiery eyes.

"They are just checking us out," Adam told the others. "We are in their land. So they want to see what we are doing."

"But we mean no harm," said Charlie.

"No," said Adam. "So they will soon go away."

After a few minutes the coyote and wolf became tired of waiting and trotted off.

Meanwhile, Adam and the Neanderthals waited and listened.

Hearing nothing but the wind, rustling bushes, and calls of birds, they moved a little closer. They settled in between some large rocks that were like a doorway to the hills beyond.

"Are we in the right place to look?" Eddy wanted to know.

Adam reassured him. "Yes. The footprints ended near here. So this is where he came to the rocks."

The Neanderthals settled back down again. It was a little like waiting by one of many entrance to a building, knowing this is where a person entered and then waited in the vast lobby, while deciding where to go next.

As the minutes ticked by, the Neanderthals heard the hooting of owls, the chatter of birds in the trees, the flapping wings of flying birds, and the chirp of crickets. Sometimes they heard one animal call to another. But nothing suggested that the escapee was even there.

Meanwhile, with the sun gone, the desert air was getting colder and colder, while the wind was blowing more strongly. The Neanderthals shivered a little and pulled their rabbit fur jackets from their backpacks. They put them on, and moved closer to each other to keep warm.

"Just keep waiting," Adam reassured them, knowing they were getting tired, impatient, and bored just waiting in silence.

Then, he noticed a few wisps of smoke rise high in the sky. They glowed slightly from the light of the moon.

"That's it!" he announced. "Maybe smoke from his campfire. He wants to get warm, too."

Adam got up and motioned for the others to follow him. Slowly, the Neanderthals moved on, very quietly as they walked with bare feet, toughened by years of growing up without wearing shoes. They walked between the rocks or scrambled over them.

Meanwhile, the wisps of smoke grew fatter and longer, as they got closer, perhaps 50 yards away. Now Adam and the other Neanderthals could smell the musky scene of burning wood.

"We're getting close," Adam said.

But as they came within 25 yards and Adam was certain the prisoner was there, he told the others to spread out.

"We want to surround him," he whispered.

Then, with a few hand signals, he told Brad to go behind him. He motioned for Charlie and Derrick to go to the right, and Eddy and Frank to go to the left.

"You go there, and I'll keep moving forward," he said quietly.

Then, keeping the rising smoke in view, the Neanderthals spread out, taking positions about 20 yards from the smoke and slowly, quietly, closing in.

Since they could no longer speak, the Neanderthals used bird calls to signal to each other -- one hoot to indicate they were in position, two hoots to indicate they were moving closer, three hoots to indicate they were even closer. They moved much like the Neanderthals might close in to trap a bison or mammoth, but now they were surrounding a prisoner, and they carried some ropes in their backpacks if needed to tie him up to bring him in. They knew not to charge in for the kill and spear the prisoner to death.

After about 20 minutes, Adam felt they were close enough to rush in and spring their trap. He could even hear the prisoner moving logs in the fire.

So he gave the signal -- four long hoots. At once, the Neanderthals all ran silently toward the prisoner, like a pack of stealthy running wolves.

Closer and closer they all came -- 15 yards, 10 yards, 5 yards.

Now they saw the burning fire and the man huddled in blankets by the fire. It seemed like it would be an easy attack. In moments the six of them could surround him, grab him, and throw their ropes around him. Then, they could force him to walk with them down the mountain and back to the desert where Lt. Davis and the sergeants would be waiting.

But suddenly, crack! Derrick stepped on a branch, which snapped with a crackle.

At once the prisoner looked up in the direction of the sound and pulled out his gun. Then, he began shooting.

Derrick heard the loud pop of the gun and fell to the ground, as the bullet tore into the tree behind him. Seconds later, another gunshot and another followed, plowing into a nearby bush and then smashing against the rock next to him.

Derrick had never heard gunshots before, and the Neanderthals had never gotten any training on what to do if someone shot at them. So he cowered motionless on the ground, afraid to move, not sure what to do next. He just knew that whatever was shooting at him was very powerful and something he couldn't do anything about. He just knew, as he saw the nearby trees and bushes quiver with each loud whizzing sound, that he had to avoid whatever it was. So he held on tight to the earth beneath him. He hoped that the shooting would stop and he would still be alive when the shooting was over.

CHAPTER 11: FIGHTING ON

After several minutes, the shots aimed at Derrick stopped, though he lay still for several more minutes, afraid to stand up and face more shooting.

Meanwhile, Adam hooted to Brad, Charlies, Eddy, and Fred to see if they were all right. Yes, they hooted back, we're fine, and he hooted back to tell them to wait.

Then, Adam had an idea. He picked up a stone and threw it, so it crashed to earth about 10 feet away. At once a series of shots rang out, aimed at wherever the rock had fallen. When the shooting stopped, Adam stealthily moved closer and threw another rock. Again, there were more shots at the rock target, followed by another few minutes of silence, and he moved closer yet.

After he threw the third rock, Adam crept over to where Eddie and Fred stood behind bushes to his left. He saw them waiting in the moonlight, and as soon as he came close, he whispered: "Throw rocks. Aim them far away."

Eddie and Fred quickly threw the rocks about 10 feet in either direction. When more shots rang out hitting several trees and rocks, Adam smiled and whispered. "Good. We know where he is. Throw more rocks and tell Brad."

As Eddie threw rocks, Fred slowly and stealthily walked to where Brad was hunkered down behind some bushes. At the same time, Adam snuck back to where he had been.

When Charles and Derrick realized what the others were doing, they began to throw rocks, too, that landed far to their left or right. At the same time, they all crept closer and closer to the prisoner by the fire. 20 feet, 15 feet, 12 feet.

Soon they could see the prisoner by the campfire holding his gun and aiming wildly, scared that an army of soldiers were coming toward him and getting closer and closer, as the pounding of what sounded like boots stomping became louder and louder.

Only 10 feet away, and the Neanderthals could see the sweat pouring down the prisoner's forehead. 8 feet away, and the pounding for the prisoner was even louder. Louder! Louder!

Finally, the prisoner stood up and threw down his gun.

"Don't shoot. Don't shoot. I'll surrender. I'll go with you," he yelled. "I don't want to die."

He stood shaking, a lone figure by fire, the flames flickering across his belly, while the moonlight shone on him like he was lit by a spotlight on stage.

At this, Adam gave another hoot. In moments, all of the Neanderthals surrounded the prisoner. They grabbed ropes from their backpacks, draped them around him, and pulled them tight, while the prisoner shook and shivered all over.

"You come with us," Adam said.

"Yes. Yes," said the prisoner, who couldn't see the Neanderthals as well as they could see him. So he thought they were regular cops or prison guards who had caught him.

"Wherever you want," he added. "I'm tired of running. I'm cold. I'm tired. I'm ready to go back."

Adam smiled broadly. "Okay. We take you back now."

Then, with Adam leading the way, Brad and Charlie on either side, and Derrick, Eddy, and Fred bringing up the rear, the Neanderthals led the prisoner back down the rocky mountain and across the desert.

In the distance, they saw Lt. Davis and the sergeants waiting for them.

Adam waved and hooted. "We back. We back."

Lt. Davis could barely believe it. The Neanderthals and the prisoner were returning so quickly and so peaceably.

He turned to Sgt. Burrows and Sgt. Garrett.

"Can you believe it? They did it. They really did. Dozens of police officers and guards couldn't find the prisoner, but they did."

"Yeah," said Sgt. Burrows. "And if they did that, just think what else they might do."

"I know," said Lt. Davis. "Let's think about that. Let's think about our other unsolved cases and what else we can do."

THE NEXT STORIES IN THE SERIES

In the next stories in the series, the New Force Neanderthals are called upon for other assignments. At first, they are recruited to track down criminals who have fled into remote areas. Then, they are hired to go after criminals who have taken refuge in factories, warehouses, abandoned buildings and boats. Later, then when hackers threaten individual computers and even the whole planet, the Neanderthals are recruited to go after them, since the methods of modern technology have failed.

Along the way, the New Force Neanderthals not only have to overcome human obstacles, but after a while, they are facing criminals who have created their own team of Neanderthals, who are helping them commit crimes.

If you like this first story, let us know, and we'll let you know when the next books in the series are published.

ABOUT THE AUTHOR

GINI GRAHAM SCOTT, Ph.D., J.D., is a nationally known writer, consultant, speaker, and seminar leader, specializing in business and work relationships, professional and personal development, social trends, popular culture, science, and crime. She has published over 50 books with major publishers. She has worked with dozens of clients on self-help, popular business books, memoirs, and film scripts.

She is the founder of Changemakers Publishing, featuring books on work, business, psychology, self-help, and social trends. The company has published over 150 print and e-books and over 100 audiobooks. She has licensed several dozen books for foreign sales, including the UK, Russia, Korea, Spain, and Japan.

She has received national media exposure for her books, including appearances on *Good Morning America, Oprah,* and *CNN.* She has been the producer and host of a talk show series, *Changemakers,* featuring interviews on social trends.

She brings to *Neanderthal* a special interest in current social trends and new developments in science and technology. Her books in this area include:

The Science of Living Longer: Developments in Life Extension Technology (Praeger) (also turned into a documentary: *The New Age of Aging,* released in June 2019*)*

The Very Next New Thing: (Praeger)

Back to the Middle Ages (AKA: The New Middle Ages - Nortia Press)

Lies and Liars: How and Why Sociopaths Lie (Skyhorse Publishing)

Scammed: Learn from the Biggest Consumer and Money Frauds (Allworth Press).

She also brings her considerable skills as a scriptwriter and executive producer of nine features, documentaries, and TV pilots, which are in distribution, release, or post production through joint ventures with Changemakers Productions. The most recently released include *Driver, The New Age of Aging, Infidelity, Me, My Dog, and I,* and *Reversal.*

She has developed stories in writing memoirs for clients. Among those which have been published are:

At Death's Door with Sebastian Sepulveda (Rowman & Littlefield) (also turned into a TV pilot *Death's Door* and documentary *End of Life*)

From School to War: Growing Up in Hitler's Germany by Wolf Dettbarn (Truman State)

American Justice? with Paul Brakke (TouchPoint Press) (the first of 9 books from American Leadership Books)

She brings to the project an extensive experience in marketing, sales, and promotion, and has turned this hands-on experience into a series of books, including:

Create a Shopify Store to Showcase and Sell Any Products (Changemakers Publishing)

Increase Your Impact and Influence (Changemakers Publishing)

Creating Your First Sales Team (Changemakers Publishing)

Work With Me (Davies-Black Publishing)

Survival Guide for Working with Humans ...Bad Bosses...Employees (AMACOM)

Scott additionally does workshops and writes books about writing and self-publishing to help other writers publish their books. These books include:

How to Find and Work with a Good Ghostwriter

Self-Publishing Secrets

Self-Publishing Your Book in Multiple Formats

Make More Money with Your Book

Conducting a Monthly Social Media Video Campaign

Conducting a Monthly Social Media Campaign on Four Major Platforms

Scott is active in a number of community and business groups, including the Lafayette, Pleasant Hill, and Walnut Creek

Chambers of Commerce. She is a graduate of the prestigious Leadership Contra Costa program and the member of several business networking groups. She does workshops and seminars on the topics of her books and on self-publishing.

She received her Ph.D. from the University of California, Berkeley, and her J.D. from the University of San Francisco Law School. She has received five MAs at Cal State University, East Bay, most recently in Communication.

OTHER BOOKS IN THE NEANDERTHAL SERIES

The Neanderthals Are Back

Who Are the Neanderthals, Really?

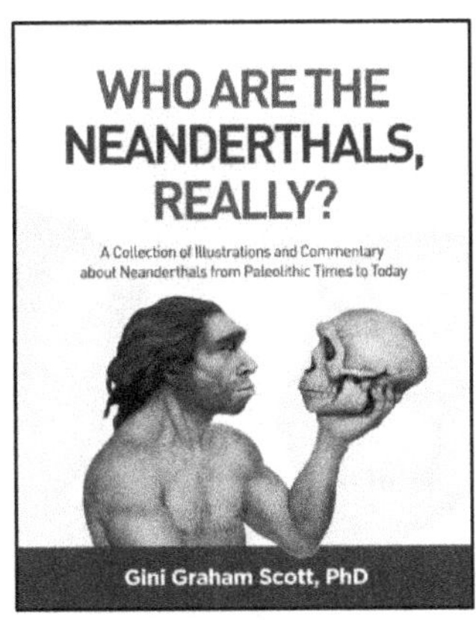

CHANGEMAKERS PUBLISHING
3527 Mt. Diablo Blvd., #273
Lafayette, CA 94549
changemakers@pacbell.net . (925) 385-0608
www.changemakerspublishingandwriting.com

www.ingramcontent.com/pod-product-compliance
Lightning Source LLC
Chambersburg PA
CBHW070453170726
48291CB00005B/1737

* 9 7 8 1 9 4 9 5 3 7 3 1 4 *